Layla's Head Scarf

By Miriam Cohen

Illustrated By Ronald Himler

Published in the United States of America by Star Bright Books, Inc.,
30-19 48th Avenue, Long Island City, NY 11101.

The name Star Bright Books and the Star Bright Books logo are registered
trademarks of Star Bright Books, Inc. Please visit www.starbrightbooks.com.
For bulk orders, please email orders@starbrightbooks.com

Hardback ISBN-13: 978-1-59572-177-8
Paperback ISBN-13: 978-1-59572-178-5

Printed in China 9 8 7 6 5 4 3 2 1

Library of Congress Cataloging-in-Publication Data

Cohen, Miriam, 1926-
 Layla's head scarf / by Miriam Cohen ; illustrated by Ronald Himler.
    p. cm.
 Summary: New in first grade, shy Layla is reluctant to participate in class activities because she feels
her head scarf makes her look too different from her classmates.
 ISBN 978-1-59572-177-8 (hard back : alk. paper) -- ISBN 978-1-59572-178-5 (paper back : alk. paper)
[1. Clothing and dress--Fiction. 2. Self-confidence--Fiction. 3. Prejudices--Fiction.
4. Interpersonal relations--Fiction. 5. Schools--Fiction.] I. Himler, Ronald, ill. II. Title.
PZ7.C6628Lay 2009
[E]--dc22
                                        2009004693

Dedicated to Laura Jackson, Shelia Kapur,
Jessie Staub, and Sandra Vizcaino at P. S. 27,
and Elizabeth O'Brien at P.S. 84.

— M.C.

First Grade sat in a circle.
They sang, "Where is Sara? Where is Sara?"
And Sara sang back, "Here I am! Here I am!
Very glad to see you, very glad to see you. Here I am!"

Jim was next. Then Anna Maria.
Everyone had a turn in the circle until it was Layla's turn.
"It's your turn, Layla!" they all said.
But Layla shook her head.

"She's shy because she's new," Jim whispered to Paul.
The teacher smiled at Layla and sang, "We're very
glad to see you, very glad to see you. Yes, we are!"

"It's library time!" said the teacher.
"Walk! Don't run!" she called.
 Everybody walked very quickly down the hall.

First Grade loved library time. They could pick any book they wanted to read. Jim was interested in turtles.

"Look at this giant turtle! It's 50 years old."

"So what?" Danny said. "My uncle is 60 years old."

"But your uncle is not a turtle," said George.

Everybody at the table laughed.

Danny asked, "Why don't you take your hat off, Layla?"
"It's not a hat. It's a scarf," Anna Maria said.
"She doesn't have to take it off if she doesn't want to."

Danny sat down next to Willy and Sammy. He showed them his book, *The World's Great Soccer Stars*.
"I'm a good soccer player," he boasted.
Willy and Sammy said, "We like baseball better.
We're for the Mets. Who are you for?"
"Shhh," said the librarian.

Anna Maria was looking at *Puppies*.
"Aren't they cute? I love puppies."
"I love kittens," said Margaret.
George said, "My gramma has a kitten. She lives
in Chicago. Sometimes I go there for
vacation and . . ."
"Where is your book, George?" the librarian
asked.

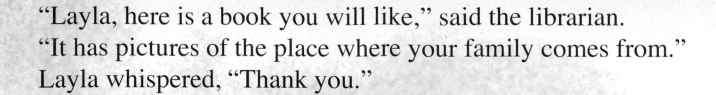

"Layla, here is a book you will like," said the librarian.
"It has pictures of the place where your family comes from."
Layla whispered, "Thank you."

The librarian held the book up for everyone to see.
It had pictures of a sandy, sunny land.
The trees were tall with tops like green feathers.
And there were lots of ladies with scarves.

After library, Danny shouted, "Lunch time!"
The lunchroom was as noisy as ten Dannys.
Everybody was talking and laughing and eating.
Danny waved his pizza singing, "Pizza, pizza, I love you!"

Layla had brought lunch from home.
It was a little pie with rice and peas inside.
"Mmm, that looks good," the lunch lady said.

Everybody ran outside for recess after lunch.
"Layla, come and play with us," Anna Maria
called. She shook her head.
"She's shy," said Anna Maria.
"Maybe you could play better if you take
your scarf off," Margaret said.

She and Sara ran to hang upside down
on the jungle gym.
Layla watched.

In the afternoon, First Grade worked on their art
project in the hall. It was called "Our Families."
Everyone had a space to paint.

Jim worked next to Sara.
He told her, "This is me, and this is my mother,
and my father, and my grampa. He's a fun grampa.
I like him to tell me stories about when he came to America."

"Why is he wearing that little black hat?" Sara asked.
"That's because he's Jewish. I don't have to wear the
hat, but I'm still Jewish."

"That's me and my dad," said Margaret.
"He always takes me to baseball games and I keep the score."

"This is me and my mama. She's doing my hair," Anna Maria said. "My daddy has to go to the barber shop to get his hair fixed."

Everybody was finished.
But Layla kept on working.
The kids went over to see her picture.
She had painted three ladies with scarves on their heads.

Layla had written, "MOMMY," "AUNTY,"
and "BIG SISTER" next to them.
A tall man held a little girl's hand.
Layla wrote, "MY DADDY AND ME."

"Why are they wearing those hats?
They look funny," Danny said.
Anna Maria said, "I already told you.
They are not hats.
They are scarves!"
"They still look funny," said Sammy.

"You shouldn't say somebody looks funny," Jim said.
"Anybody can look like they want to! This is America!"
"Who says so?" asked Danny.
"My grampa!" Jim answered.

Danny tried to tell them, "I didn't say *they* were funny-looking.
I said their scarves look funny."

Layla was trying not to cry. But one tear came, and then another.
"Now look what you've done!" Anna Maria scolded.
"You've made Layla cry!"
"Don't cry, honey, " Sara and Margaret said.
And George said, "Your mommy looks like a really nice mommy."

Their teacher came to see if they were working hard.
Jim said, "Look! Layla drew such a nice
picture! All of the ladies are wearing
pretty scarves like Layla's."
"It's beautiful," said the teacher.
Layla stopped crying and smiled
for the first time that day.

The next morning, First Grade sat in their circle.
Each one took a turn. When they sang, "Where is Layla,
Where is Layla?" she sang back, "I am here! I am here!"

Danny was going to tell her, "You're *supposed* to say, 'Here I am, Here I am,'" but he didn't.
And everybody in First Grade clapped and clapped for Layla.